BENNY
The Bunny

The True Meaning of
Christmas & Easter

To Cecily

but God Bless You

Love

Copyright © 2019 James "Jim" Allen Dowell

All rights reserved. Except as permitted under the U.S. Copyright Act of 1976,
no part of this publication may be reproduced, distributed, or transmitted in any form or by any means,
or stored in a database or retrieval system, without the prior written permission of the publisher.

For information or permissions write:

James "Jim" Allen Dowell

jdmanagement@ymail.com

Writer: James "Jim" Allen Dowell

Illustrator: Jerry Pittenger

Printed in the United States of America

First Edition: October 2019

ISBN Paperback 978-1-7007065-7-7

This book is dedicated to my wonderful parents,
Lullie Mae and Bill Dowell, for teaching my brother John
and me the true meaning of Christmas and Easter.

Benny is an Easter Bunny who is brown with big floppy ears. He never liked his floppy ears much though. He thought they were just too big.

Benny didn't like Easter much either because
his mom and dad made him hide Easter Eggs –
those yellow, baby blue, and pink Easter Eggs.
He also didn't like the color pink and thought it
was not very cool for a bunny to be hiding eggs.

What Benny really loved was Christmas!
It was his favorite time of year. He loved the
snow, all the beautiful colored lights, the decorated
Christmas trees, and most of all, he loved Santa.

His goal in life was to be a reindeer. Benny wanted antlers, majestic antlers. He wanted to fly through the sky delivering beautiful red and green wrapped presents to good little girls and boys all over the world.

Yes, Benny thought that being a reindeer would be the greatest! So one Christmas he came up with a plan to trick Ole Santa.

He bought antlers that looked more like moose horns and tied them on his head with shoestrings. He bought a paste on nose with a bright red glow and he bought, what he thought were reindeer paws, that he could slip on over his own feet.

On Christmas Eve Benny was ready to put his master plan into action. He had always wanted to guide Santa's sleigh, so dressed in his reindeer outfit, he made his way to the North Pole.

There in front of him was a magical site. It was Santa's shiny red sleigh filled with wonderful toys and his magnificent reindeers all hitched up and ready to fly.

Finally, Santa was leaving his workshop with the last of the beautifully wrapped presents.

Benny knew he must hurry! So he ran as fast as he could to the front of Santa's sleigh, hitched himself into the harness, and waved to Santa that he was ready to go.

The event he had dreamed of all his life was finally here.

At that moment, Santa cracked his whip and yelled. "On Dasher, on Dancer, on Prancer, and Vixen. On Comet, on Cupid, on Donner, and Blitzen!"

Santa's sleigh began to slide and leave the ground. It was more than Benny could've ever imagined. He was FLYING! The air was cold but there was a warm feeling in his heart.

The sky was filled with snowflakes, like flying through diamonds, but suddenly Benny's excitement came to an end. He realized that he was afraid of heights. That warm fuzzy feeling turned into out and out fear!

He began to cry, "Help Santa Help!
It's me Benny and I'm afraid!"

Santa, knowing all the time it was Benny, turned the sleigh around and landed safely back at the North Pole. Once on the ground Santa unhitched Benny from the harness, took him to the sleigh, put him on his lap and said, "Ho, Ho, Ho, Benny! That was quite a ride!"

"Yes Santa," Benny said crying. "I'm sorry but I've always wanted to be a reindeer and go with you on Christmas Eve. I didn't know it was going to be so scary!

"I'll tell you what's scary, Benny," Santa said. "It's your reindeer outfit. Your antlers look more like moose horns, the red nose is not that bright, and reindeer have hooves not paws."

"I guess I do look a little silly, Santa," Benny said, "but all my life I have loved Christmas." That's when Santa smiled, hugged Benny, and told him a story he would never forget.

"You know Benny, Christmas is a wonderful time of year. Families come together, children wait for me to bring them toys and gifts, and all over the world there is a feeling of peace on Earth, good will toward men."

"But most important of all Benny, Christmas is the time of year we celebrate the birth of the Baby Jesus. The Lord our God sent His only Son here to Earth to be our Savior."

So you see Benny, that's the true meaning of Christmas. Now, let me tell you about Easter. For Easter is just as important as Christmas.

"Easter is just as important as Christmas? Benny asked. Yes Benny," Santa replied.

"Easter is the time of year we recognize the death of Jesus on the Cross, and we celebrate His resurrection from the tomb. Jesus died to save us all from our sins. Now all we have to do is believe in Him and we can have everlasting life."

"You should never want to be something you're not and you should be the best Easter Bunny you can be."

From that night on Benny loved Easter. He loved hiding Easter Eggs for all the Children and seeing their happy faces.

He even liked the color Pink a little more, but most of all he like being an Easter Bunny.

He was now proud of who he was and his mission in life became telling children of all ages the true meaning of Christmas and Easter.

Made in the USA
Monee, IL
20 November 2020

48720697R00021